in

Study Hard, Play Fair & Help Others

Written by Coach Dave Irby

Illustrated by Rebecca Santana

Meet your new friends.

As we prepare for our story, Sammy Surge has just been reunited with his long-lost twin brother Ralph. Sammy Surge and Ralph were separated at birth and Ralph had been living on the streets, which is where Grampa Smitty found him. Sammy Surge was adopted by Grampa and Grama Smitty, who are always taking in *lost boys*, including Sammy Surge's soccer coaches—Hansi and Matumbu—when they were little. Grampa and Grama Smitty have now taken Ralph into their home, and along with Sammy Surge, they hope they can help Ralph with his anger issues, learn how to behave in school, play on a soccer team without cheating and live with his new family. They hope they can help Ralph learn to *study hard, play fair and help others!*

Chapter 1 - Study Hard

It was late Friday afternoon, and Sammy Surge, his brother Ralph, and all the kids in Mr. Schulz's fifth-grade class were *impatiently* waiting for the school bell to ring. Mr. Schulz quieted the class down, "Before you leave for the weekend, just a reminder that the theme for your story is due on Monday morning."

Sammy Surge immediately looked over at Ralph, worried that Ralph might get angry again. Well, sure enough, Ralph let out a loud grunt that the whole class heard, causing Mr. Schulz to pause, then say, "Relax. It's just your *theme* and to make it easy you just need to write your two to three paragraphs on *I have learned it is always best to be someone who BLANK*. You decide what goes in the blank." Just then, the school bell rang! Ralph stomped out of the classroom before Sammy Surge, or the other kids finished writing it down.

When Sammy Surge got home, Ralph was already playing video games. Sammy Surge decided it would be a good idea to write his theme that day because he and Ralph had a soccer game the next day, and he didn't want to have to be thinking about it the rest of the weekend. He also knew he wouldn't have time to write it after the game because the coaches were going to take the team out for ice cream! As Sammy Surge began to write, Ralph came into the kitchen. "What are you doing?" demanded Ralph.

"I'm doing my homework," Sammy Surge answered.

"What homework?" questioned Ralph.

"The theme for our story Mr. Schulz told us to write for Monday."

"OH NO!" shouted Ralph angrily, "boring, boring, boring! Anyway, we have all weekend to write it." Ralph grabbed a bag of potato chips and went back to his room.

The next morning Sammy Surge was up early putting the finishing touches on his paper. "There, I'm finished," Sammy Surge said to himself. Then he called out to his brother, "Hey, Ralph, you better get up and get something to eat; we need to leave for our game."

Ralph stumbled out of bed. "Okay, okay, I'm up."

Today was the final day of the regular season for their Surge FC Junior team and

Sammy could already see that Ralph was sad. "Listen, Ralph, I know you are worried that you might not play much today because of the way you have acted in some of our games. But each of the last two games you have played a little bit more because you have not yelled at the referee or made any bad fouls. You just must trust Hansi and Matumbu, they are really fair coaches."

Well, Ralph wasn't in the starting lineup again, but instead of stomping around or pouting, Ralph went up to Hansi and Matumbu and said, "I'm ready if you need me."

Five minutes after the game started, Hafeni had to come out because he wasn't feeling well. "Ralph, you are going in for Hafeni." Well Ralph played the rest

of the game, scored two goals and played hard AND he didn't get into any trouble!

At the ice cream parlor after the game, Hansi and Matumbu spoke to the team. "Congratulations on winning the game, and now we get to play in the League Championship game next week.

More importantly, you all showed good sportsmanship."

The next day, Sunday, was a difficult day; while Sammy Surge went with Grama and Grampa Smitty to church, Ralph was back to his "old tricks," pretended to be sick – moaning, grunting and snorting like he was going to die. Ralph stayed in his room all day, probably playing video games, thought Sammy. But each time Grampa or Grama Smitty or Sammy Surge knocked on his door and opened it, there was Ralph lying in bed, acting like he was sick.

On Monday morning at school, Mr. Schulz collected the students' homework, but one was missing. It was Ralph's. Mr. Schulz said, "I'm sorry, Ralph, but you will not be able to go out to play at recess time this week; instead, you will be writing your theme while the other kids are out playing." Ralph immediately crossed his arms and started pouting, but then Sammy Surge gave Ralph that look, that only Sammy could do, and that made Ralph feel ashamed. Then "*poof,*" it was like a light bulb went off in his head, and he found himself saying to Mr. Schulz, "I know what the theme of my paper is going to be:

I have learned that it is always best to be someone who **Studies Hard**.*"* Mr. Schulz smiled and gave Ralph a high five at the same time as Sammy Surge was giving his brother a hug.

For why it is important to **Study Hard** go to **www.SammysTeam.com**. *You will also find Sammy Surge poster & Video.*

Chapter 2 - Play Fair

"I can't find my shin guards!" yelled Ralph. "I've looked everywhere. Where could they be?" Sammy Surge calmly walked over to his brother and pointed. Ralph looked down and asked, "What are you pointing at?"

Sammy Surge smiled and said, "Look at your shins." In his rush to get ready for the game, Ralph forgot that he was so excited last night about the game that he had slept with his shin guards on. Once Ralph looked down and saw his shin guards and then looked at Sammy Surge, they both fell on the ground laughing and crying at the same time.

Today's game was for the league championship. Sammy Surge and Ralph's team were playing the defending champions, the Red Dragons. Sammy Surge and Ralph's team, the Surge Juniors, had been training very hard, and the team's coaches, Hansi and Matumbu, thought they had a good chance of winning and Ralph had a good week in school and at soccer practice.

When they arrived at the soccer field, Sammy Surge was picked to be the team's captain and participate in the coin toss, and when Hansi announced the starting lineup, Ralph's name was called; then Matumbu reminded the team, "remember we always play to win the game, and to win the Fair Play award."

Next, the referees and team captains met for the coin toss. Sammy Surge said, "Hi" and tried to shake the hand of the Red Dragons' captain, but he just gave Sammy a dirty look.

Sammy Surge won the coin toss, and the Red Dragons' captain whispered, "That's the only thing you will be winning today; we are going to crush you!"

Sammy Surge just stood there, not sure how to respond.

Then the referee said, "Let's have fun and play fair today."

As the game began, it was clear that the teams were evenly matched. The Red Dragons scored first, but Ralph was playing "out of his head," and just two minutes later Ralph scored the tying goal on an amazing bicycle kick!

At halftime, the teams were still tied at 1-1. As the Surge team gathered for the halftime break, Hansi said, "Great goal, Ralph."

Matumbu added, "We know the other team is playing pretty rough; don't let that keep you from playing the right way."

In the second half, the play became more intense. The Red Dragons didn't like the way the game was going, so they began to foul the Surge Juniors' players even more. Sammy Surge could hear the Red Dragons' coaches telling their players "foul them, kick them!" Halfway through the second half Sammy Surge hit a great shot that banged off the crossbar, just before the Red Dragons' captain stomped on Sammy Surge's ankle forcing Sammy Surge to limp off the field in obvious pain.

Because the game was still tied at the end of regulation time, the teams had to play two five-minute overtime periods.

With just three minutes left to play, Coach Hansi put Sammy Surge back into the game. Sammy Surge's ankle was still hurting, but he really wanted to play. Sammy Surge had an immediate impact on the game as his first pass was a great pass to Ralph, who dribbled into the penalty box and pushed the ball past two Red Dragons' defenders; then suddenly – Ralph fell down and started rolling around and yelling like he was in pain. The referee didn't really see what had happened, but with Ralph rolling around and screaming the ref panicked. He blew his whistle and pointed to the penalty spot. The defenders around Ralph yelled, "Ref, we didn't touch him!" and the Red Dragons Coaches were screaming at the top of their lungs at the referee, who was only fifteen years old. It looked like the Surge Juniors were going to win the championship. But from his position in midfield, Sammy Surge saw that his brother Ralph might be pretending that he had been fouled.

While Ralph was rolling around, Sammy limped up to him, leaned over and whispered something in Ralph's ear. Ralph immediately stopped rolling around and yelling and everyone else stopped. There was complete silence on the field and the sidelines. Ralph uncovered his eyes and looked up at the referee and said in a shaky voice… "I, I, I'm sorry; the defenders did bump into me and tried to trip me, but I kind of tripped over my own feet too - it shouldn't be a penalty kick." The referee was very impressed with what Ralph said and with Sammy Surge's sense of fair play. The Red Dragons' captain was overwhelmed with emotion. He shook Sammy Surge's hand and helped Ralph up, as Ralph was injured during the play; and because Sammy Surge was having trouble walking the Red Dragons' Captain even helped him over to the sidelines.

After the game ended, the League Officials called everyone over for the awards presentation. The Red Dragons' coaches surprised everyone by asking Hansi and Matumbu if the whole Surge team could join them in front of all the parents and spectators. The Red Dragons Coaches again surprised everyone by asking Sammy Surge and Ralph to stand next to them while the Red Dragons received the Championship awards. The Awards officials and everyone else were confused by what was taking place. Then Coach Brent from the Red Dragons said, "Even though the Surge Juniors lost the match in the penalty kick shootout after overtime, I am ashamed at the way I asked my players to play today, and I will never do that again. I would like to present our coach's Championship medals to Sammy Surge and Ralph because they are the true heroes of the game because they showed everyone the importance of **Fair Play**!"

Learn more about **Fair Play** @ www.SammysTeam.com
You will also find Sammy Surge poster & Video.

Chapter 3 - Help Others
a few months later

"Are you awake?" whispered Ralph.

"Yes," whispered Sammy Surge right back.

"I can't sleep. I'm just too excited! I still can't decide between the black or blue ones." After a moment's silence, Sammy could hear Ralph quietly sniffling. Sammy reached out his hand and patted his twin brother. Ralph responded by saying, "I still can't believe Grama and Grampa Smitty would take me in. I've caused them and you so much trouble with my outbursts in Mr. Schulz's class and kicking people on the soccer field and yelling at the refs. Sammy, you are always so calm and help me when I am out of control. I can't believe that Grama and Grampa would buy me new soccer cleats."

"Hansi used to be kinda like you, Ralph, but Grama and Grampa and Mr. Schulz really helped him feel better about himself, and he changed. And look Ralph, you are changing; your grades are getting better, and you are really doing so much better on the soccer field and in Mr. Schulz classroom. Let's try and get some sleep or Grama, and Grampa might not let us have a living room sleepover again for a while."

Grama and Grampa Smitty always made great dinners. Grama made sack lunches for Ralph and Sammy Surge to take to school, and Saturday was usually the day that Grampa Smitty made his special breakfast - pan size giant pancakes with bacon and eggs. Ralph and Sammy loved Saturdays, but today they ate super-fast so they could get to the soccer store right when it opened.

"I like the red ones!" exclaimed Ralph.

"Those are nice, but I've decided to get these blue cleats," said Sammy Surge.

The brothers were so excited about their new cleats that they raced to the park and try them out. As Ralph hit a curling ball to Sammy Surge, he said, "Did you see that? I've never been able to curl a ball like that before. These new cleats make me so much better. I love them!"

Sammy Surge agreed, "I think you're right, Ralph."

Just then, a few kids from Sammy Surge and Ralph's school arrived at the park. Jericho said, "hey, do you guys want to play some soccer?"

"Absolutely!" shouted Ralph.

Hafeni said, "cool, Danny and Jericho, why don't you guys pick the teams," but after picking, one team was short a player. Sammy Surge noticed a little boy standing by himself near the goal, so Sammy went

over and asked if he wanted to play soccer with them. The little boy seemed so very happy that he was asked.

"Thank you. I love to play soccer. My name is Marcos." Sammy Surge, Ralph, and the rest of the kids introduced themselves to Marcos, but they couldn't help but notice that Marcos was wearing dirty old cleats with broken shoelaces and several holes in each shoe.

Sammy Surge and Ralph were playing great soccer. They both agreed that their new cleats had improved their game. However, little Marcos was at a completely different level from the rest of the kids. His soccer touch was amazing, and his ability to score goals was ridiculous!

After the game, the other kids left for home, but Sammy Surge, Ralph and Marcos stayed behind to juggle. Sammy Surge asked Marcos if he played on a team. Marcos told him that his dad had lost his job so they couldn't afford to get him cleats, and that's why he couldn't play on a real team.

"That's too bad. Well, we gotta get home. Let's go," said Ralph.

Sammy Surge told Marcos that he'd be right back, and then he went up to Ralph and said, "Ralph, what are you doing? Marcos needs our help. He needs some cleats."

"I knew you were going to say that. That's why I said we should leave. I'm not giving a stranger my new cleats," admitted Ralph.

"I didn't say you had to give him your new cleats," said Sammy Surge. "I just want to think of a way we can help him." The two thought for a few minutes, and then Ralph had an idea, their soccer coaches Hansi and Matumbu collected old discarded cleats and kept them in their garage. Maybe they'd have a pair for Marcos.

Sammy Surge walked back and asked Marcos if he'd like to play soccer the next afternoon. Marcos said he would.

That night Grama and Grampa Smitty had Hansi and Matumbu over for dinner. After another delicious meal, Hansi opened up a bag with ten pairs of used cleats. "Here," said Matumbu, "pick a pair for your new friend Marcos. After Sammy and Ralph decided on a pair, Hansi explained to them, that Grampa Smitty had taught him and Matumbu how important it was to transform them from old cleats into a special present. So, with Hansi and Matumbu's guidance, Sammy and Ralph cleaned them up, and when they had dried, they polished them, so they looked like new. They even took out the old shoelaces and put brand new ones in.

When Marcos arrived at the park the next day, Ralph handed Marcos a nicely wrapped box. Sammy Surge said, we have a present for you, go ahead and open it. Marcos opened the box and couldn't believe what he saw; he was so happy; he almost began to cry. "Thank you so much. Now I can play on the team!"

Sammy Surge got choked up and Ralph, with a tear in his eye, had to admit, "It sure makes you feel good to **Help Others**."

Learn more about **Helping Others** at: www.SammysTeam.com
You will also find Sammy Surge poster & Video.

More on Sammy Surge

So many people around the world love soccer, or football, as the rest of the world calls it – so we thought it was time for you to meet Sammy Surge. Sammy is the warm and fuzzy mascot fox for Surge International, a wonderful group of soccer teams, coaches, players, referees, and fans all over the world. Sammy Surge is an inspiration to the young and young at heart. As a Global Ambassador for the Surge, Sammy Surge has entertained soccer fans at stadiums; visited school children in Oregon, California, and New Jersey; participated in annual Christmas parties for homeless children and visited orphans in Mexico. Sammy Surge has even stopped off at Manchester United and taken photos with Man U's Fred the Red at Old Trafford and spent time in one of his favorite countries, Austria, where he has visited two of his favorite cities, Vienna and Salzburg. In Salzburg, he was the special guest of the famous Red Bull Salzburg Soccer Team and their mascot Bullidibum at their Fan Day.

Fun Facts

Sammy Surge once visited six elementary schools and 3,000 school children in New Jersey in one day, and his teammates conducted 80 school assemblies for 40,000 children in six weeks! Over 150,000 school children have seen their special performances, including two schools in Salzburg, Austria.

Sammy's teammates have now visited forty-three countries.

Sammy Surge has visited an orphanage in Mexico several times. His teammates visited with children from a blind orphanage in Peru. *Sammy Surge and his friends love children all over the world!*

Sammy Surge's **downloadable mini-poster is free,** and you can watch his **video** with Hansi and Matumbu too!

Just go to @ www.SammysTeam.com

Surge Soccer is for players, coaches, referees and fans who believe in the power of soccer to help make a better world!

*Since Sammy Surge is from the United States, we are using the term **soccer**, which of course is called football around the world. Our English version is geared towards readers in the United States, with the hopes that others around the world will enjoy the story, despite some slight differences in the English language.

**Sammy Surge is grateful for the Manchester United Foundation and the photos taken with Fred the Red, and for Red Bull Salzburg allowing Sammy Surge to participate in their Fan Day with Bullidibum and their team and fans but *No endorsement of this book and its content should be implied.*

See so much more about Sammy Surge and his pals on

Instagram @ **surge_soccer** and at www.SammysTeam.com

Contact our wonderful Illustrator –
Rebecca Santana @ rys.empathy@gmail.com

Surge Soccer is for players, coaches, referees and fans who believe in the power of soccer to help make a better world!

David Irby, Author

Since earning a US Soccer 'A' Coaching License and an M.A.T. (University of La Verne, CA) Dave has crisscrossed the globe to over 40 countries as a soccer coach. Dave and his teams have been ambassadors through soccer to little jungle villages and national soccer stadiums, and impacted orphans and whole countries. Dave is the inventor of Sammy Surge and the founder of Surge International, a 501 c 3 non-profit organization. He has coached at all levels, including: youth teams with the LA Galaxy OC, Timbers Academy (Salem, OR); three high schools, three universities and the D2 Southern California Seahorses. He has shared his story and vision for "hope" around the world.

Full biography is at: www.surgesoccer.org (under Directors) book Dave to speak to your group or to invite Sammy Surge to your next event @ dirby@surgesoccer.org

Stay tuned—there could me more!   Just email info@surgesoccer.org for updated Sammy Surge information and travels.

No mascots were injured in the writing of this book.

ACKNOWELDGEMENTS

For my mom and dad, Jack and Lois Irby, who taught me to love God, family and country. My dad who taught school and worked at Disneyland the first year that it opened. My mom, who raised her four boys, John, David, James and Mark, and taught us to love to read.

With special thanks to Coach Chip Fuller, who helped with the writing of this book. Meet Chip @ www.chipfuller.com

Melissa Kaye, expert content editor and Writeralways16, copy editor, translated into German by dear friend Güner Can from Salzburg.

For Amber Smart, who formatted the cover and interior. ambersmartdesigns@gmail.com

All my colleagues at Surge and around the world; Azusa Pacific University for starting a soccer team that helped me fall in love with soccer, and Trinity United Presbyterian Church (Santa Ana, CA) for teaching me that helping people is one of the keys to life.

And of course, my wife Susie, who has stood beside me as I have traipsed to forty-three countries; coached multi soccer teams; traveled to dangerous places, and mostly for her being long-suffering with my random ideas and preoccupied brain.

And to my children, Nathan, Ryan and Hayley who had to put up with my crazy antics and sometimes feeling that Sammy Surge was my most important child.

Mehr über Sammy Surge

So viele Menschen auf der ganzen Welt lieben Fußball – deshalb dachten wir, es wäre Zeit für dich, Sammy Surge zu treffen. Sammy ist das kuschelig niedliche Maskottchen für Surge International: eine wundervolle Gruppe von Fußball Mannschaften, Trainern, Spielern, Schiedsrichtern und Fans aus der ganzen Welt. Sammy Surge ist eine Inspiration für die Jungen und die Junggebliebenen. Als ein globaler Botschafter für Surge, hat Sammy Surge in Stadien schon viele Fußballfans unterhalten. Er besuchte Schüler in Oregon, Kalifornien und New Jersey, nahm an alljährlichen Weihnachtsfeiern für heimatlose Kinder teil und besuchte Waisen in Mexiko. Sammy Surge hat sogar beim Manchester United Halt gemacht und machte Fotos mit Man U`s Fred the Red in Old Trafford. Er verbrachte außerdem Zeit in einem seiner Lieblingsländer, Österreich, wo er zwei seiner Lieblingsstädte Wien und Salzburg besuchte. In Salzburg war er der besondere Gast des berühmten Red Bull Salzburg Fußballteams und ihrem Maskottchen Bullidibum an ihrem Fan-Tag.

Lustige Fakten:

Sammy Surge besuchte einmal sechs Volksschulen und 3000 Kinder in New Jersey an einem Tag. Seine Teamkollegen führten ihn in zu 80 Schulveranstaltungen für 40.000 Kindern innerhalb von sechs Wochen! Über 150.000 Schulkinder, darunter zwei Schulen aus Salzburg, haben ihre Spezialaufführungen gesehen.

Sammys Freunde haben bis jetzt 43 Länder besucht.

Sammy Surge hat schon öfters ein Waisenhaus in Mexico besucht. Seine Kameraden besuchten ebenfalls Kinder in einem Blinden Waisenhaus in Peru. *Sammy Surge und seine Freunde lieben Kinder auf der ganzen Welt!*

Sammy Surge`s downloadbares Mini-Poster ist gratis und du kannst sein Video mit Hansi und Matumbu hier anschauen!

Geh zu: @ www.SammysTeam.com

Surge Fußball ist für Spieler, Trainer, Schiedsrichter und Fans, die an die Kraft des Fußballs glauben und Surge will dadurch helfen, eine bessere Welt zu schaffen!

*Da Sammy Surge aus den USA stammt, benützen wir den Ausdruck Soccer, was natürlich überall auf der Welt mit Fußball übersetzt wird. Unsere englische Version ist für Leser in den USA gedacht, in der Hoffnung, dass andere rund um die Welt auch die Geschichte genießen, trotz mancher kleiner Unterschiede wegen der englischen Sprache.

**Sammy Surge bedankt sich bei der Manchester United Foundation und für die Fotos, die mit Fred the Red gemacht wurden und bei Red Bull Salzburg, die Sammy Surge erlauben, an ihrem Fan-Tag mit Bullidibum und ihrem Team und mit den Fans teilzunehmen. *Keine Vermarktung des Buches oder dessen Inhalten wird dadurch impliziert.*

Viel mehr über Sammy Surge und seine Freunde gibt`s auf Instagram @surge_soccer und auf www.SammysTeam.com

Keine Maskottchen oder kleinen Kinder sind beim Verfassen dieses Buches zu Schaden gekommen.

Made in the USA
Columbia, SC
20 June 2023